JON SCIESZKA'S TRUCKTOWN

KAT'S MAPS

BY JON SCIESZKA

CHARACTERS AND ENVIRONMENTS DEVELOPED BY THE

DAVID SHANNON   LOREN LONG   DAVID GORDON

ILLUSTRATION CREW:

Executive Producer:

TOT
INDUSTRIES

Creative Supervisor: Nina Rappaport Brown ○ Drawings by: Dan Root ○ Color by: Antonio Reyna
Art Director: Laura Roode

Ready-to-Read

Simon Spotlight

New York   London   Toronto   Sydney

SIMON SPOTLIGHT

An imprint of Simon & Schuster Children's Publishing Division

1230 Avenue of the Americas, New York, NY 10020

Copyright © 2011 by JRS Worldwide, LLC.

For information about special discounts for bulk purchases, please contact Simon &
Schuster Special Sales at 1-866-506-1949 or business@simonandschuster.com.

Manufactured in the United States of America 0511 LAK

First Simon Spotlight edition, June 2011

10 9 8 7 6 5 4 3 2 1

Library of Congress Cataloging-in-Publication Data

Scieszka, Jon.

Kat's maps / by Jon Scieszka ; artwork created by The Design Garage: David Gordon,
Loren Long, David Shannon. — 1st Simon Spotlight ed.

p. cm. — (Jon Scieszka's Trucktown) (Ready-to-read)

Summary: Kat, who loves to make maps of all sorts of places and things, gives a special
map to Jack.

[1. Maps—Fiction. 2. Drawing—Fiction.] I. Design Garage. II. Title.

PZ7.S41267Kas 2011

[E]—dc22

2009046920

ISBN 978-1-4169-4148-4 (pbk)

ISBN 978-1-4169-4159-0 (hc)

Kat makes maps.

Kat makes maps
of her room,

maps of her block,

my house

flower box

N

B

Dumptruck
Dan's

Pete's
house

CONSTRUCTION
site

my
house

pipes

mel's
house

maps of her town,

and maps of her world.

Kat loves maps.

Kat makes maps of her mind

and maps of her heart.

"Here is a map for you,"
says Kat to Jack.

"Where does it go?"

"To a surprise."

Jack follows Kat's map.

He turns right on Bumper Street.

He turns left on
Motor Lane.

Jack drives over Speed
Highway.

Under Race Bridge.

"Aha," says Jack.

"I should have guessed."

"An art show of all . . .

. . . Kat's maps."

31901050703141